Bjrnstjerne Bjrnson

A gauntlet, being the Norwegian drama en hanske

Bjrnstjerne Bjrnson

A gauntlet, being the Norwegian drama en hanske

ISBN/EAN: 9783337303723

Printed in Europe, USA, Canada, Australia, Japan

Cover: Foto ©Andreas Hilbeck / pixelio.de

More available books at **www.hansebooks.com**

A GAUNTLET

BEING THE

NORWEGIAN DRAMA

EN HANSKE

BY

BJÖRNSTJERNE BJÖRNSON

TRANSLATED INTO ENGLISH BY

OSMAN EDWARDS

LONDON

LONGMANS, GREEN AND CO.

AND NEW YORK: 15 EAST 16TH ST.

1894

PREFACE

On January 20, 1894, 'A Gauntlet' was thrown down on the stage of the Royalty Theatre. Its clang evoked responsive applause from no small part of the audience, unanimous disapproval from the critics. To account for their verdict, one need not accredit Mr. H. L. Brækstad with membership of a Moonlight Club. His widely-known translation of the author's first version naturally misled his fellow-critics, ignorant of the second, into a supposition that the adaptor had taken the most unlicensed liberties with the text. Admirers of Norwegian drama have a right to know exactly what those liberties were. My own wish was to present the play as it stood, with little or no modification. If London playgoers were equal to Ibsen, undiluted Björnson would not prove too strong for them. But I had reckoned without the stage-manager. Not satisfied with ruthless omission, this potent intermediary interpolated some lines, and so effectually changed others, that the general effect was to turn a grave comedy into a semi-serious farce. The character of Mrs. Ries was soured ; the carefully directed 'curtains' robbed of effect. In its final shape 'A Gaunt-let' was sent to the author, who replied that he could not spare time for supervision, and that I must take all responsibility. Reducing the demand for excision to a minimum in view of the late stage of the rehearsals, I was refused, and had no option but to submit the play, as 'adapted' by Mr. George Hawtrey, to its other executioners. It will not surprise me, however, if the inclement veteran (of *The Daily Telegraph*) and the witty *franc-tireur* (of *The Star*) agree for once in regarding Björnson as his own executioner, since most of their strictures apply to his 'second thoughts,' here faithfully set forth.

A complete appreciation of the play is, perhaps, impossible, without some knowledge of its birth, its re-birth, its relationship to other offspring of the same parentage. It was born, then, in Paris in 1883, and had for twin-

brother 'Pastor Sang' (Over Ævne). To
produce in one year two plays, which challenged
so directly the religious and ethical ideas of
his countrymen, was characteristic of the
author, then at the zenith of his 'second youth,'
as Georg Brandes styles the most strenuous
decade (1873-83) of Björnson's life. During
that period he turned from the fashioning of
exquisite poems, saga-plays, and peasant-tales,
from the romantic fatherland of Grundvig and
Wergeland, to grapple with social problems in
seven dramas of modern life. Of the earlier
five, two—'The Editor' and 'The King'—
took as their *milieu* the political world; two
—'A Bankruptcy' and 'The New System'—
the commercial; one, entitled 'Leonarda,'
portrayed the duel between an emancipated
woman and a bishop-ridden community. If
'Pastor Sang' may be regarded as in some
measure a result of the religious controversy,
in which the author engaged before leaving
Norway in the autumn of '82, it is equally
certain that the atmosphere of Paris was not
without effect on the spirit and form of 'A
Gauntlet.' Too sure an artist to load his

drama with didactic matter, Björnson un-
burdened his soul four years afterwards in a
lecture—'Polygamy and Monogamy'—which
was delivered in more than sixty Scandinavian
towns, and of which more than 80,000 copies
were sold in a threepenny edition. He did
not mince words about French 'lubricity.'
'Look at the otherwise self-respecting, puncti-
lious Frenchman ! when passion seizes him, he
loses all those qualities, all power of resistance :
an abyss yawns before him, and into it he
falls. . . . The great writers of France have at
last discovered this abyss, and one may say,
that the stench of what is now being drawn
from its depths pervades the world.' It had
invaded Norway, where Hans Jæger had
made a bid for Zola's laurels by publishing
'From the Kristiania-Bohême,' and the Government had confiscated Kristian Krog's novel—
'Albertine'—a plea for the emancipation of
Nana from state control. Thus men's minds
were ripe for the poet's denunciation of the
unrecognised 'polygamy,' which was sapping
'the fine sensibilities of youth, the fertility of
talent, family life and national character'; for

his remedial advocacy of bolder education, greater facility of divorce, the opening of more employments to women, and the equalisation of the sexes. It is well to note how strongly Björnson, the reformer, sympathises with such ideals as those of which Svava is the champion ; for his sympathies do not prevent Björnson, the artist, from depicting with impartial power worldly sense and unworldly aspiration, the outraged cynic and the disillusioned girl. His direction to play the comedy lightly, 'as if it had no *tendenz*,' is of a piece with the supreme naturalness of the characters. Nowhere is the dramatist hampered by the pulpiteer.

In 1887 the play was rewritten in the shape, and with the lineaments, which the present translation has endeavoured to reproduce. The first act had been little altered, but the second and third were entirely recast ; one prominent character had been omitted, and the ending was totally changed. It remains, therefore, to append a brief outline of the first version, since comparison of the two sheds interesting light on the author's constructive methods.

ACT I

Mrs. Ries is discovered in conversation with 'Uncle Nordan,' an old friend of the family, who informs her that Mr. Christensen has advanced money to satisfy Mrs. North, and. will expect repayment from Ries. The exposure of the latter is thus prepared from the first, whereas in the second version no hint is vouchsafed, until Mrs. Ries says (in Act II.): 'I could answer you if I chose. You count on my silence.' The playful and serious scene between Svava and her parents, the talk of the lovers, the revelation of Alf's past by Hoff, are practically identical in both versions.

ACT II

Svava is successively urged by her mother, father, and Dr. Nordan to forgive Alf. She reproaches the first with inconsistency, and recalls an episode of her childhood, when she had found her mother crying and been told: 'Never give way in what you know to be good and pure, for it always means giving way more and more!' Nordan begs her to take time and not decide hastily on a 'doubtful question discussed by serious men and women all over the world.' She replies impetuously: 'It only concerns me, and there's no doubt about it.' Soon after Mr. and Mrs. Christensen call; a family council is held; the lovers are sent for. Alf is humble and conciliatory, but when the issue is put plainly to him: 'A woman, then, owes a man her past and future, but a man only owes a woman his future?' he assents. The indignant girl dashes her glove in his face.

NORDAN

That was a gauntlet!

CHRISTENSEN

It is war, then? Well, I understand a little about war.

ACT III

Early on the following morning Alf comes haggard and sleepless to Dr. Nordan's house, where he begs permission to remain in order to see Svava. He is followed by his father *en route* for the palace to be presented with other knights of St. Olaf. Then Mrs. Ries arrives, and a sharp logomachy ensues. To old Christensen's disgust Alf refuses to take up the gauntlet. 'I love her more than ever,' he declares, 'whatever she may think of me.' It appears that Mrs. Ries has written a letter overnight to her daughter, telling her of her father's infidelity. As a result, Svava is more inclined to relent towards Alf, but cannot quite forgive her mother. 'I should have been told before; when I was old enough to understand.' To his deeply distressed wife and child Ries now enters, full of childish delight in the decoration, which Christensen has procured for him—an unexpected move in the family-war. Unable or unwilling to perceive their suffering, he goads Svava into the despairing cry: 'You have ruined my home for me; almost every moment of the past seems tainted!' The final scene between the lovers ends as follows :—

ALF

May I ask one thing,—one thing, with all my heart?—*Wait for me!* We two have planned out

our life, and I will carry out the plan . . . alone.
Perhaps, one day, when you see how faithful I
have been . . . Give me an answer. I must have
something to live for ! Give me a sign ! Reach
out a hand to me !

> [*Svava turns and reaches out both hands. He
> goes.*

MRS. RIES

Did you promise him something?

SVAVA

I think so.

> [*Clings to her mother in great agitation.* ·

O. E.

DRAMATIS PERSONÆ

Ries.

Mrs. Ries.

Svava Ries, their daughter.

Christensen.

Mrs. Christensen.

Alf Christensen, their son.

Hoff.

Marie, servant in Ries's house.

Peter.

Hanna, Kamma, Frederike, and three other
young girls.

Action takes place in Ries's house.

A GAUNTLET

THE FIRST ACT

A tastefully arranged music-room. In the background, open doors, leading into a park; on either side of the doors, windows; busts on the intervening walls. On the right are windows; on the left two doors, of which the first leads into Ries's room; between the doors, rather forward, a piano: in front of it a music-stool. In the foreground, on both sides, sofas; in front of the right-hand sofa a small table, chairs, a music-cabinet between the windows on the right, etc.

THE FIRST SCENE

Mrs. Ries; immediately after, Ries. Mrs. Ries is seated on the right-hand sofa, with her face turned to the park, a magazine in her hand, which she reads from time to time during the following scene. Ries enters from his room. He is in his shirt sleeves, and is fastening his collar.

A

RIES

I haven't seen Svava yet.

MRS. RIES

Svava has gone out.

RIES

Gone out?

MRS. RIES

To the baths.

RIES

Oh!
[*Crosses to the windows on the right, then vanishes again into his room, but comes back at once, and again crosses to the windows, busied all the time with his collar.*

MRS. RIES

Perhaps I can help you?

RIES

Oh dear no! Thanks all the same! These new shirts give one no end of trouble. I bought them in Paris.

MRS. RIES

Yes,—a whole dozen, wasn't it?

RIES

And a half. When did you come home last night ? I did not see you leave.

MRS. RIES

No, you were playing cards ; we did not wish to disturb you. About one o'clock, I should think. And you ?

RIES

Not much before half-past two. What a large party it was !

MRS. RIES

Yes ; but not on a luxurious scale ; rather stingy, I thought, for a betrothal-party.

RIES

I am told that was Alf's wish.

MRS. RIES

Alf is opposed to luxury. Tell me, how do you like him ?

RIES

Very much. There can't be two opinions about *him*.

   [*He again vanishes into his room and comes back.*

Do you know, I 'm racking my brains over a problem ?

It must be very complicated.

To be sure, to be sure! So it is. This collar is simply. . . . There! at last!
[*Goes again into his room and returns, this time with a tie in his hand.*
What I 'm puzzled by is our dear girl's character.

Svava's character?

Yes; I 'm wondering what traits she has from you, and what from me; or, rather, what traits she inherits from your family, and what from mine, and so forth. Svava is a remarkable girl.

She is indeed.

Taken as a whole, she is neither you nor I, nor even a combination of both.

MRS. RIES

No, Svava is something more.

RIES

Yes : ever so much more.
[*He vanishes again and returns, this time in
his coat, which he brushes from time to
time.*
What do you say ?

MRS. RIES

Nothing.   Only, Svava is like my mother.

RIES

Well, I must say! Svava's quiet, pleasant
disposition—what are you dreaming of ?

MRS. RIES

Svava can be passionate enough.

RIES

She never sets convention at defiance, as
your mother did.

MRS. RIES

You never understood my mother.   But I
dare say they are different in many things.

RIES

I should think they were!   Now, do you
see that I was right to reason with her ever

since she was quite little? Do you see that, now?—you objected at the time.

I objected to your perpetually plaguing her —there was no end to it—first one thing, then another.

Yes, but the result, my love? the result?
[He begins to hum.

Well, you surely won't say your arguments made Svava what she is?

[*Vanishing into his room again.*] Not only the arguments but—[*from his room*] the arguments had a great deal to do with it! Did you notice her yesterday? She has plenty of *savoir vivre.* What? *[He comes out again.*

Surely, that is not what we prize most in Svava?

No, no! On the steamboat a man asked me if I were related to the Miss Ries who founded the Orphanage here. Yes, I said, I had the honour to be her father. You should have seen the fellow then! I was quite touched!

MRS. RIES

Yes,—the Orphanage has been a success from the first.

RIES

Was it through the Orphanage that she became engaged?

MRS. RIES

You had better ask Svava.

RIES

But you're not noticing me at all—my new suit?

MRS. RIES

Indeed I am!

RIES

Haven't you a word of admiration? The *tout ensemble*—a harmony in colour, eh?— down to the very shoes! And the pocket-handkerchief to match!

MRS. RIES

How old are you, Ries?

RIES

Hush! hush! Well, how old do you suppose people would take me for?

MRS. RIES

For forty, of course.

RIES

'*Of course*'? As if it were so self-evident! Let me tell you, this suit is a sort of Festal Overture, composed in Cologne directly I received the telegram about Svava's engagement. Think of that!—in Cologne! not ten hours' journey from Paris! But I couldn't wait ten hours—I was so impressed with my own importance, when I thought that my daughter was about to marry into the richest family in the country.

MRS. RIES

Did you only buy that suit?

RIES

What a question! Wait till my trunks come from the Custom-house!

MRS. RIES

Ah! then it will be our turn, I suppose!

RIES

Your turn ? Very fortunate for papa—wasn't it ?—to be on his way to Paris at the critical moment !

MRS. RIES

Yes : and you nearly missed the party altogether.

RIES

Oh ! but that was splendid—as it turned out—the steamer being so late—for suddenly —as if a magician had waved his wand,—there was I in the middle of a *fête champêtre* ! A party in honour of my own, my only daughter —where, naturally, I had a most flattering reception. Never in my life had I been so fêted before.

MRS. RIES

Who did you play cards with ?

RIES

Can you believe it ? I made up a rubber with Abraham, Isaac, and Jacob ? In other words, with our host, the Minister of State, and my brother, the Director-General. It 's an exceptional honour for a man to lose his money to such distinguished persons,—for I invariably lose. What 's that you 're reading ?

MRS. RIES

The Fortnightly.

RIES

Has there been anything in the last number or two while I was away ?

[*Begins to hum a tune.*

MRS. RIES

Yes, here is an article on the very subject we 've been discussing,—hereditary transmission.

RIES

Do you know this tune ? [*He crosses quickly to the piano.*] There 's a rage for it just now. I heard it all over Germany. [*He plays and sings a few bars, but breaks off suddenly.*] I 'll fetch the music before I forget.

[*Dives into his room and returns with a piece of music. He seats himself at the piano and continues to play and sing.*

THE SECOND SCENE

The same. Svava enters by second door on the left.

RIES

[*Stops at sight of her and jumps up.*] Good

morning, my dear girl, good morning! I've
scarcely had a chance of saying 'How do you
do?' yet. I couldn't get near you at the party.
[*He kisses her, and advances with her to the
foreground.*

SVAVA

Why were you so long returning from abroad?

RIES

Why don't people give notice when they
intend to be engaged?

SVAVA

Because they know nothing about it themselves until it happens. Good morning again,
mother! [*She kneels beside her.*

MRS. RIES

Ah! how fresh and sweet you are! You
went into the woods after your bath?

SVAVA

[*Rising.*] Yes, and on my way home I met
Alf, who wished me good morning. He'll
be here in a minute. [*To Ries.*] And do you
know what *I*'ve seen? Do you know what
vessels are in the harbour?

RIES

Aha! have they arrived at last? My two large yachts?

SVAVA

Yes, they're close to the bridge! The deck is like the floor of a ball-room.

RIES

Don't you think one might dance on it?

SVAVA

What a splendid idea! No one but you thinks of such things! Fancy! two large boats side by side, with one deck laid over both, and an awning above——

RIES

And in front a steam tug with a band on board, and then out to the fiord!—Hurrah!

SVAVA

Every one I've spoken to means to have an awfully jolly time to-morrow. As for me, I feel as excited as a child.

RIES

To tell the truth—which one should always

do—I had quite given up all idea of ever seeing our ' little old maid ' so happy.

SVAVA

Yes, indeed ! so had I.

RIES

Until this prince came ?

SVAVA

Until this prince came. He was a long
time coming.

RIES

Was he ? And did you have to wait all that
time ?

SVAVA

No, certainly not. I never gave him a
thought.

RIES

That sounds mysterious.

SVAVA

Yes, it is mysterious how two people, who
have known one another from childhood,
without giving each other a thought, suddenly
—for that is how it was—became totally dif-

ferent. Since one particular moment, Alf hasn't seemed the same person to me.

RIES

While, of course, to the rest of the world he is unchanged?

SVAVA

I hope so.

RIES

Anyhow, he is much livelier—I can see that.

SVAVA

Yes, I saw you laughing together yesterday. What were you laughing at?

RIES

Can't you guess? At the lady who had the place of honour next his mother.

SVAVA AND MRS. RIES

[*Throwing away the magazine.*] Ah! 'the Dragon'!

RIES

Yes. Were they making fun of any one else?

MRS. RIES

To me she is the most repulsive person in the world, with her knitting-basket, her pug, and her mischievous tongue.

RIES

Oh! but when you're the richest member of the family, and an old maid, people only think you original. We laughed at everything she said, and thought it very witty.

MRS. RIES

Well, there was a limit to my patience—I came away.

RIES

Yes, I noticed that. You belong to a different cult. Those who worship the Golden Calf have a hard time of it. No one is so dependent as the rich.

MRS. RIES

[*To Svava, who is looking out of the window.*] But what actually passed between *you* and her?

RIES

Between you and 'the Dragon'? Was anything the matter?

SVAVA

She was very kind ; she is always kind to me.

MRS. RIES

Yes, but you left her rather abruptly. She must have said something ?

RIES

About me ?

SVAVA

If you must know, she said something disagreeable about Alf.

RIES

About Alf.

SVAVA

'Disagreeable' is not the right word, perhaps. She said, 'If at any time you want to know anything about your *fiancé*, just come to me.'

RIES

She's a troll ! a wicked troll ; for there are good trolls too. And, talking of them, let me congratulate you on your new morning dress. Under the circumstances it is really stylish.

SVAVA

Under the circumstances ? Does that mean, considering *you* could not be with me to choose it ?

RIES

Yes : for I should never have chosen this trimming—though, under the circumstances, it's not so bad. And the cut ? Dear me Just wait till my trunks come !

SVAVA

Surprises ?

RIES

Splendid surprises ! Stop ! I have something here as it is. [*Goes into his room.*

SVAVA

[*To Mrs. Ries.*] He's very restless, mamma, —more than usual. Don't you notice it ?

MRS. RIES

He's so pleased, my child ! So delighted to be home again——

SVAVA

But there's always something so gentle and winning about papa . . .

Ries comes back.

SVAVA

[*To him.*] Do you know what the Minister of State said about you yesterday?

RIES

What a man of such high position says must be worth hearing.

SVAVA

' Miss Ries, your father is still our man of fashion—*par excellence !* '

RIES

Ah, son excellence a bien dit! But I can tell you something better than that. You shall make your father *decoré*——
[*He points to his button-hole.*

SVAVA

I ?

RIES

Yes, who else ? Already the Government has been of use to me more than once in various business transactions:—but this time

I shall accept the order of St. Olaf.
[*Describes a cross on his breast.*

SVAVA

I congratulate you!

RIES

'When it pours on the pastor, it rains on the clerk,' you know. As father-in-law of our great man——

SVAVA

You are really so uncommonly modest in your new capacity.

RIES

Am I not?—And now I will appear in the character of a modest Exhibitor of elegant costumes—or rather, of designs for costumes —a still more modest *rôle*!

SVAVA

Oh no, papa! Not now!

MRS. RIES

Don't let us begin with them till the afternoon!

RIES

Really, any one would believe *I* was the only

woman in the house! Well, as you will. For I have another proposal in two parts.— Part 1: Let's sit down!

SVAVA

We will.   [*They seat themselves.*

RIES

[*To Svava.*]   Now that papa has come home, tell him exactly how it all happened. Explain that mystery, you know!

SVAVA

Oh! indeed! No, you must excuse me. I can't tell you!

RIES

Not with its tender details! Good heavens! Who would be so brutal as to ask? Before you have been engaged a month! No: I only meant how you came to know each other.

SVAVA

Oh! for that I have to thank our precious Orphanage.

RIES

Your precious Orphanage, you mean?

SVAVA

No : we have more than a hundred girls interested in it now.

RIES

Well, go on : so he came with a subscription ?

SVAVA

Yes : with several.

RIES

Aha !

SVAVA

One day we happened to speak of luxury. We thought it so much better to spend time and money in a good cause than on luxury.

RIES

Well, but what do you mean exactly by 'luxury' ?

SVAVA

We didn't define it, but I said that I considered luxury immoral.

RIES

Immoral ?—luxury ?

SVAVA

Yes: I know that is not *your* view, but it is *mine*.

RIES

Your mother's, you mean, and your grand-mother's.

SVAVA

Quite so: but mine too—if you have no objection?

RIES

Heaven forbid!

SVAVA

I was telling him of something we saw in America—you, mother, and I—don't you remember? We were at a temperance meeting, and saw some ladies drive up, who came to support Moderation! Those ladies—well, we didn't know the amount of their fortunes, but to judge from their horses, toilets, and jewels—especially jewels—they must have been worth——

RIES

Many thousand dollars!

SVAVA

And that is just as much one form of excess as drunkenness is another.

RIES

Well, and what then?

SVAVA

Ah! you shrug your shoulders. Alf didn't shrug his. He began to tell me of his experiences . . . in the large towns.

RIES

His experiences?

SVAVA

Yes: of the gulf between rich and poor, between boundless want and shameless luxury.

RIES

Really! . . . I thought . . . Well, go on!

SVAVA

He didn't sit unconcerned, trimming his nails——

RIES

I beg your pardon!

SVAVA

Pray, don't disturb yourself! No; he prophesied a social revolution, and spoke with the utmost fervour. Then he explained his opinions about private property. It was all so unexpected, so novel to me. You should have seen how noble, how beautiful he looked!

RIES

Really? beautiful?

SVAVA

Yes: at least *I* thought so. And so did mother. Didn't you?

MRS. RIES

[*Continuing to read.*] Yes, dear.

RIES

Mothers are always in love with their daughters' accepted suitors! But that soon passes off, when they become sons-in-law.

SVAVA

Is that *your* experience?

RIES

That is *my* experience. So Alf Christensen has grown beautiful? I suppose I must agree with you?

SVAVA

As he stood there,—steadfast, frank, and pure—for he must be that too!

RIES

What do you mean by 'pure,' my dear girl?

SVAVA

I mean what the word means.

RIES

Exactly: what does it mean?

SVAVA

Well, it means, what I hope any one would understand by it when applied to myself.

RIES

What?—The word has the same meaning to you—neither more nor less—whether used of a man or a woman?

SVAVA

Yes, of course.

RIES

And you imagine that a son of Christen-sen——?

SVAVA

[*Rising.*] Father, you hurt me!

RIES

How can Alf's being his father's son hurt you?

SVAVA

In this point he is not his father's son! I am not deceived in him!

MRS. RIES

I'm just reading about inherited qualities. He need not be an exact copy of his father.

RIES

Well, well, as you will! I fight shy of all your air-spun theories. They never carry you any further.

SVAVA

What do you mean?

RIES

Don't be so excited! Come and sit down! Besides, how can you know?

SVAVA

How can I know——? What?

RIES

Why, in each particular case——?

SVAVA

How do I know if a man, with whom I associate, is a man or a brute?

RIES

Ah! There we have it. You may be mistaken, my dear Svava. Come and sit down!

SVAVA

No; I am no more mistaken in him than I am in you, papa, when you tease me with your horrible principles. For, in spite of all you say, you are the most refined and delicate . . .

MRS. RIES

[*Throwing away the magazine.*] Are you going to keep on that dress, my child? Won't you change it before Alf comes?

SVAVA

No, mother, it's no use trying to turn the subject! Too many of my girl friends have repeated the old story of Beauty and the Beast with this difference.—In their case the lover . . . began by being a Fairy Prince, but when they awoke from their dream he was transformed into a beast. I won't have anything like that! I won't make that mistake.

MRS. RIES

Well, you needn't speak so vehemently. Alf is an honourable young man.

SVAVA

Yes, he is. But I have come across so many shocking cases. And only the other day there was that affair of Helga Holm!

MRS. RIES

Yes, that was dreadful.

RIES

What was that?

SVAVA

Haven't you heard?

RIES

No.

SVAVA

They are separated.

RIES

The Holms?

SVAVA

For unfaithfulness.　　She discovered her husband——

RIES

The devil!　Recently?

SVAVA

Quite recently.

RIES

Hm !　Well, well !

SVAVA

And now I will tell you something, which I have never spoken of before.　Do you know that once—long ago—I was very nearly engaged ?

RIES AND MRS. RIES

[*Rising.*]　You, Svava ?

SVAVA

Yes.　I won't say to whom !　I was very, very young, and he professed—oh ! the noblest principles, the highest aims !　In this respect he was exactly the opposite of papa.　To say

I loved him would be too little. I worshipped him! But you must excuse my telling you what I discovered, and how. It was at the time when you all believed I was——

MRS. RIES

Consumptive?

RIES

Was it then? [*Svava nods.*

MRS. RIES

[*Approaching her.*] And you never told me a word?

[*Ries goes towards the left.*

SVAVA

Well, it's all over now! But one thing is quite certain; when a woman has once had such an experience, she will not let herself be deceived twice.

[*Ries has meanwhile disappeared into his room.*

MRS. RIES

Perhaps it was for your happiness, after all.

SVAVA

Yes, I am convinced of that! Well! it's all over now! But my sufferings were not en-, tirely over until I found Alf. Where is papa?

MRS. RIES

Papa? Here he comes.

RIES

[*Comes out of his room, with his hat on, in the act of drawing on a glove.*

Now, children, I must go to the Custom House to see after my trunks. Good-bye, my dear girl! [*Kisses Svava.*] You have made us very happy, very happy! But some of your ideas . . . well, well! [*Going off.*] Good-bye!

MRS. RIES

Good-bye!

RIES

[*Coming back once more, to Svava, while he again draws on his glove.*

Did you notice that tune I was playing just now? In Germany I heard it everywhere. [*He begins to play and sing, but suddenly he jumps up.*

No, I spoil it.   However, there's the music;
you can learn it for yourself.

[*He retires to the back, humming.*

SVAVA

He is delightful!   There is really something so artless about him.—Did you notice
him yesterday?   He was quite brilliant!

MRS. RIES

I wish you could have seen yourself!

SVAVA

Yes.   I was happy!   Why should I deny it?
Every one was so kind, yes, everybody!

[*She embraces her mother.*

MRS. RIES

Now I must look after the housekeeping a
little.

SVAVA

[*Accompanying her.*]   Shall I help you?

MRS. RIES

No; stop where you are!

SVAVA

Well, I'll play over papa's tune once or

twice—it is really pretty—and very soon Alf
will be here !

> [*Mrs. Ries passes out of second door on the*
> *left. Svava takes her seat at the piano*
> *and begins to play.*

THE THIRD SCENE

Svava. Alf enters on the right from the back.

ALF

> [*Comes softly up and leans over Svava, so*
> *that his face almost touches hers.*

Thank you for yesterday !

SVAVA

Alf ! I didn't hear you ring.

ALF

Your father met me at the door. What a
pretty tune that is !

SVAVA

Yes. And thank you, thank you *so* much
for yesterday.   [*They retire to back together.*

ALF

You can't imagine what a success you were.

SVAVA

Perhaps I can—just a wee bit.

ALF

Every one is delighted at home.

SVAVA

So they are here.

ALF

If even 'the Dragon' thought you 'splendid,' you can judge what an impression you made !

SVAVA

Really ?   I fancied I had offended her.

ALF

Oh dear no !   But I saw you left her rather abruptly.

SVAVA

Oh, that was nothing !   What have you in your hand ?   A letter?

ALF

Yes.   Your maid gave it me.   Some sharp

fellow has found out that I should come here in the course of the morning.

SVAVA

You think that was not hard to guess ?

ALF

Not very.   I must go over to see Edward Hansen.

SVAVA

You can take a short cut through the park.
[*She points to the left.*

ALF

I know.   And as he writes '*urgent,*' and underlines the word——

SVAVA

You can have my key.   Here !
[*Giving it to him.*

ALF

Thanks ! many thanks !

SVAVA

Oh, it's purely selfish ! I shall have you back again the sooner.

ALF

I can stop here till noon——

SVAVA

Oh, longer, much longer—can't you? We have such a lot to say to each other about yesterday.

ALF

And about to-morrow too. Do you know, I hadn't seen your father's floating ball-room?

SVAVA

No? Did you ever hear of such an idea? I *shall* enjoy myself to-morrow!

ALF

I sha'n't enjoy myself in the least.

SVAVA

Is it possible? Why, everybody will.

ALF

Except me; and that is why I *do* want a talk with you. Couldn't we meet somewhere to-morrow before the party? Alone?

SVAVA

Will you come over here, then?

ALF

Yes, but wouldn't it be better if we went out for a row?

SVAVA

Just as you like.

ALF

Ah! thanks. Quite early, mind. I can't spare you a moment; and the party only keeps you away from me. Why didn't we find each other sooner?

SVAVA

Because we hadn't reached the right stage.

ALF

How can you tell? I believe we were meant for one another.

SVAVA

We suit each other very well—don't you think so?

ALF

Uncommonly well! But we can't be sure that that isn't partly the result of what we were before.

SVAVA

There ! that's what I said !

ALF

Now I must be off: the letter says '*in haste.*'
[*They retire to the back.*

SVAVA

One minute can make no difference ! Do
you know, when I saw you yesterday among
the others I didn't recognise you ? You were
quite changed. You had become some one
else.

ALF

Ah ! that's always the way, darling ! there
are some things one never sees except in con-
nection with others. *Now* I realise for the
first time how tall you are, and how, when you
bow, you bend—the least little bit—to one
side. Now I know exactly the colour of your
complexion, your hair, your neck . . .

SVAVA

Excuse me, it's *my* turn to speak !

ALF

Well, then ?
[*Both, having reached the door at the back,
turn round again and advance to the front.*

SVAVA

When you looked at me and leaned on me just now, I had such a strange sensation; I felt that I was blushing to the roots of my hair.

ALF

Really? That isn't how I felt. Whenever any one danced with you I felt mad with jealousy. Yes, you may look at me! I begrudged you to him—yes, I begrudged you to every one! My God! I can't bear any one to touch you! [*They embrace.*] But I've not yet told you what I like best of all.

SVAVA

And that is?

ALF

This.—If I saw you far off, among the others, it might be only a flying gleam of your arm, I loved to think: This arm has clung to *my* shoulder, to *my* neck, and to no other in the whole world! It is mine—it belongs to me, and to no one, no one, no one else! Why, how's this? Are we back again already? This is sorcery! Well, I must go now. [*Moves towards back.*] Good-bye!

[*Lets Svava go, and at once embraces her again.*

Why was not this happiness mine years ago?
Good-bye!

SVAVA

I think I 'll come with you.

ALF

Yes, do!

SVAVA

No: I had better practise this tune until
papa comes back. I shall have no time later
on. Good-bye, then. [*The house bell rings.*

ALF

Here comes some one! Send him off soon,
whoever he is. We want to be alone.
    [*Hastens through the left-hand door at the
        back. Svava gazes after him. She is just
        in the act of going to the piano when Marie
        enters.*

THE FOURTH SCENE

Svava. Marie. Later, Hoff.

MARIE

[*From second door on the left.*] A man is here
who——

SVAVA

Do you know him ?

MARIE

No.

SVAVA

What sort of man ?

MARIE

Well, he is rather . . . rather . . .

SVAVA

Suspicious-looking ?

MARIE

Oh dear no ! Quite a respectable man.

SVAVA

Tell him papa is not at home.

MARIE

I have told him so; but he wishes to speak to you, Miss.

SVAVA

Oh ! ask mother to come. But no, why should she ? Show him in.

[*Marie goes out through same door by which Hoff now enters.*

HOFF

Have I the honour to address Miss Ries?
Yes, I see you are she. My name is Hoff—
Karl Hoff, commercial traveller. In *iron*,
Miss, in *iron*——

SVAVA

Yes; but what have I——?

HOFF

Well, you see, if I'd been an ordinary stay-
at-home householder, like other people, a good
many things would never have happened!

SVAVA

What would never have happened?

HOFF

[*Draws out a pocket-book and takes a letter
from it.*
Will you be so kind — so kind as to read
this? Or perhaps you would rather not?

SVAVA

Well, how can I tell?

HOFF

No, of course: you must first . . . *if* you
please——   [*Hands her the letter.*

SVAVA

[*Reading.*] 'This evening between ten and eleven—that is if—"the Noodle" doesn't come home—1 love you with all my soul—Put a light in the passage window.'

HOFF

I am 'the Noodle.'

SVAVA

But I don't understand——

HOFF

Here is another !
[*He hands her a second letter.*

SVAVA

'I am conscience-stricken. Your cough frightens me, and just now, when you are expecting . . .' But what in the world has all this to do with *me* ?

HOFF

[*After some reflection.*] Well, what do you think of it ?

SVAVA

Is it some one I ought to help?

HOFF

No; she needs no help now, poor creature!
She is dead.

SVAVA

Dead? Was it your wife?

HOFF

Yes, it was my wife. I found these and one
more . . . in a little case. At the bottom lay
the letters—these are not the only ones—and
just above them was a little wadding in which
was a pair of earrings, together with a few
trinkets . . . —presents from her mother. And
then I found these bracelets—look! they are
decidedly too expensive for her mother to
have given her!

SVAVA

She died suddenly then, before——

HOFF

Well, I can't say. Consumptive people
never think they are going to die, else, no
doubt, she would have hidden all this away.
Ah! she was so gentle, so delicate! May I
take a seat?

SVAVA

Pray do! [*Hoff takes a seat.*] Are there any children?

HOFF

[*After some consideration.*] I believe not.

SVAVA

You believe not? I asked, because I thought you had come about our Orphanage. I need not say this is most painful for me!

HOFF

Yes; so I thought, so I thought! I'm not at all sure whether I . . . but there! you don't understand!

SVAVA

No, indeed I can't.

HOFF

No, no, of course not! I've heard so much good of *you* for many years; and my wife used to praise you too.

SVAVA

Did she know me?

HOFF

She was Maren Tang—she was a companion
to——

SVAVA

To Mrs. Christensen, my future mother-in-
law? So it was she? Why, she was an edu-
cated, quiet, lady-like girl. Surely you have
made some mistake? A few notes without a
signature, without even a date?

HOFF

Didn't you know the writing?

SVAVA

I? No. It's disguised, isn't it?

HOFF

Yes, but not very much, I think.

SVAVA

Had you not a special object in coming to
me?

HOFF

I had; but I think I will let it alone. I see
well enough you don't understand such things.
Perhaps you think my mind is slightly affected.
Well, it wouldn't be surprising.

SVAVA

Still, you must have had an object ?

HOFF

So I had !   You see, this Orphanage——

SVAVA

Oh ! it is about that, then !

HOFF

No, not exactly.   But it's owing to the
Orphanage that I have thought so highly of
you for a long time past—and a good many
others have done the same.   If I may take
the liberty of saying so, I never saw any
fashionable young lady before occupy herself
with something useful.   Never before.   I am
only a poor, broken-down merchant.   I have
to travel for other firms now, and I've met
with many misfortunes.   Perhaps I was to
blame for most of them.   But you see, I was
anxious that *you* should be spared !   I thought
to myself, it's incumbent on me . . . my
positive duty ! . . . But now, when I sit face
to face with you . . . I only feel that I'm
very miserable.   No, I want nothing from you,
nothing at all.

SVAVA

I don't understand you.

HOFF

You mustn't bother any more about me. I beg your pardon a thousand times, a thousand times! [*He rises to his feet.*] No, please don't trouble your head about me in the least! Forget me altogether! I have not been here. That's all!

> [*He meets Alf at the door, just as the latter is entering. When Hoff observes that Svava is looking attentively, he goes hastily out.*

THE FIFTH SCENE

Svava.   Alf.   Last of all, Ries.

Svava, who has remarked the agitation of both men, utters a muffled shriek. She hastens towards Alf, but, as soon as she has looked him in the face, staggers back in sudden horror. Alf tries to support her.

SVAVA

Don't touch me.

⌊She hastens through the second door on the left. From the outside is heard the slamming of the door and the drawing of a bolt. Then, for a moment only, violent sobbing, somewhat subdued by distance. Outside Ries is heard to hum the same tune as before, and immediately after he enters

THE CURTAIN FALLS.

THE SECOND ACT

The same room.   The afternoon.

THE FIRST SCENE

Mrs. Ries.   Marie.

MARIE

The gardener is here.   He wishes to know how soon we are to bring in the flowers and decorate the music-room.

MRS. RIES

At once ! . . . Or rather . . . I'm not quite sure, Marie.

MARIE

Well, we can't put it off any longer, m'am, if we're to have any decorations at all.

MRS. RIES

Oh ! we have plenty of time by to-morrow afternoon !

MARIE

Yes; but to-morrow there will be so many
other things to do. Oh dear, Mrs. Ries, what
is the matter? I saw Miss Svava go out just
now looking so unhappy.

MRS. RIES

Well, she must tell you herself, Marie!
[*Sits down and begins to cry. A ring is
heard at the door.*

MARIE

Perhaps that is she. [*Peeps out.*] No; it
is the ladies' trio. Must we have them now?

MRS. RIES

Oh dear! They want to practise, I suppose.
The trio is to be sung to-morrow at the party
—if there is to be one.

MARIE

[*Surprised.*] What do you say?

MRS. RIES

Svava must tell you herself! We had better
sit up late and do the work, Marie. I can't
undertake anything now.
[*The trio is heard outside.*

MARIE

Shall I tell the gardener he had better bring
the flowers to-night?

MRS. RIES

Yes, do, Marie.　　　　　*[Marie goes out.*

The Second Scene

Mrs. Ries.　The Ladies' Trio.

*Six girls enter, each with a bouquet in her hand, led
by Peter, tripping in waltz measure.　Peter
hastens at once to the piano and begins the
accompaniment.　The girls advance to Mrs.
Ries, and move about her in waltz-time, while
one couple dances round and round her.　When
they come to the words: 'Hand in hand now
turning, turning,' they form a close circle round
her.　The dance is repeated.*

WALTZ

Dawn, brightly breaking,
Blissful awaking,
When Love is born, like a flower set free,
When, in high splendour,

Magical, tender,
Venus soars up from the heart of the sea.
 Rich to completeness,
 Spring scatters sweetness ;
 Airs with glad greeting teem,
 Beckon with scent and gleam,
 Harmonies falling,
 Beauties enthralling,
Blend, reeling forth in a riotous stream.

 Hand in hand now turning, turning,
 Steals through every maid a yearning ;
 Captive we by dreams enclosen,
 Each is dreaming of her chosen,
 Dreams of wedding and of wooing,
 Love's obtaining, Love's undoing.

 Fetterless forces
 Lie at Life's sources,
Fires, that must mingle in madness of strife,
 Till, by their roaring
 Currents' out-pouring
Mightily moulded, at last blossoms life.
 Twine the wreath busily,
 Speed the dance dizzily,
Swiftly desire to fulfilment is winging.
 Lovers ! Love guide you,
 Dream-like, beside you,
On—ever on—to the sound of our singing !

ALL

Good-morning, auntie ! How are you, auntie ? How jolly it was yesterday !

HANNA

Just fancy, auntie, we kept it up until five this morning !

KAMMA *and* **FREDERIKE**

We went into the woods and sang.

HANNA

We haven't been to bed at all.

THE OTHERS

No : not one of us !

SEVERAL

We have been together all this morning !

FREDERIKE

Yes, and we saw the pleasure-boats, too !

HANNA *and* **KAMMA**

We went on board——

ALL

And danced !

HANNA

Oh, it was splendid !

FREDERIKE

Ah ! how jolly it will be to-morrow !

ALL

O auntie !

KAMMA

And now we'll practise the trio for to morrow.   Isn't the new waltz charming?

MRS. RIES

Yes, indeed.

PETER

We shall have a pretty practice to-day !

KAMMA

Peter is as cross as a bear to-day.

HANNA

Yes, odious !

ALL THE OTHERS

Simply odious, auntie !

KAMMA

You know in the waltz it says : ' Blissful

awaking, when Love is born, like a flower set free?' Well, every time he roars out '*Painful awaking!*'

ALL

Ha, ha, ha!

HANNA

He's as dull as ditch water!

FREDERIKE

He's only tired, poor fellow! He's so *blasé!* It was a shame to keep him up all night.

ALL

Poor thing!

PETER

Thank you! I appreciate your sympathy, if I am *blasé.*

HANNA

Where is Svava, auntie?

MRS. RIES

She has gone out.

KAMMA

With her *fiancé*?

MRS. RIES

No, alone.

SEVERAL

Alone?

PETER

Ha, ha, ha!

FREDERIKE *and* **KAMMA**

Be quiet!

HANNA

I can guess where she is!

ANOTHER

So can I!

HANNA

She is at Helga Holm's, auntie!

FREDERIKE

Isn't it shocking about Helga?

MRS. RIES

Indeed it is, child.

HANNA

To be so deceived in her husband!

ALL

Shocking !

MRS. RIES

Still, I wasn't altogether surprised.

FREDERIKE

Why ? Was he always like that ?

KAMMA

Before he was married ?

MRS. RIES

Yes. And, as the French say, 'Qui boit, boira.'

ALL

There, you hear that, Peter ? You hear that ?

PETER

It may be true of Holm, but not of everybody. I think you are all crazy !

MRS. RIES

No, of course it is not true of everybody. There are exceptions.

PETER

There, you hear that? You hear that?

SOME

We didn't say 'everybody'!

PETER

Yes, you did, you little geese!

ALL

'Little geese,' auntie!

MRS RIES

There are exceptions. But, as a rule, I find that either a man is faithful to one woman on principle, or else, his principles allow him to be unfaithful. At any rate, that's *my* opinion.

SEVERAL

Peter, Peter, you hear that?

HANNA

You must always be faithful, do you understand?

PETER

Fiddle-de-dee! To whom, if I'm not married?

HANNA

To yourself, stupid !

PETER

Ah ! Rubbish !

ALL

[*Except Hanna.*] Did you hear, auntie ?
Peter says ' Rubbish ! '

The Third Scene

*As before. Svava enters hastily from the Park;
on seeing the others wishes to turn back.*

PETER

Here's Svava !

ALL

Here's Svava ! [*They go to meet her, draw
her in with them, and all talk at once.*] Here's
a bouquet for you ! How charming you were
yesterday ! We have not been to bed all
night ! We have been singing in the wood.
We have been about together all day. Now
we are going to practise the trio.

HANNA

Why, Svava, what is the matter with you?

KAMMA

Is there anything wrong?

MRS. RIES

Don't you see, she has just come from Helga Holm?

ALL

[*Except Hanna.*]   Of course she has!

MRS. RIES

Helga is her bosom friend, you know.

SEVERAL

[*In an undertone.*]   So she is.

SVAVA

How lovely the flowers are!   Thank you, thank you very much!   Shall we put them in water at once, mother?

MRS. RIES

Yes, I will see to it.
   [*She touches a bell.   The maid appears, and, at a sign from her mistress, brings a basin, while Mrs. Ries busies herself in arranging the flowers during the following dialogue.*

SVAVA

How fresh and sweet they are! We must take great care of them, else they'll die, too, very soon! Yes, you're quite right; I have been with Helga Holm. Where else should I have been?

KAMMA

Isn't it shocking? The whole town is talking about it.

SVAVA

Really?

SEVERAL

The whole town!

SVAVA

Well, there'll be still more to talk about!

HANNA

Will there?

SEVERAL

Will there?

SVAVA

Yes. But that's *splendid*, that the whole

town should be talking about it ! That is as
it should be ! Every one should talk about it !
. . . Oh, I think I must go out into the air
again !

MRS. RIES

[*Who is tying up the stalks and putting the
flowers in a glass.*
Take off your hat, darling !

SVAVA

Ah ! yes : I didn't think of that.

HANNA

You look so strange, Svava !

ALL

Yes, she does.

SVAVA

Do I ? Well, I must have been out more
than two hours, and all that time I have heard
nothing but 'Tell me, tell me, tell me !' I
couldn't bear it any longer !

MRS. RIES

[*Goes hastily up to Svava.*] Come with me,
come to your room, dear ! You want rest.

SVAVA

Rest? Now? If only I could scream or cry! When you have been deceived——

MRS. RIES

[*Quickly interrupting.*] Like Helga Holm?

SVAVA

Like Helga Holm? Yes, Helga Holm! Ah! no: I must speak out. All this time I have scarcely said a dozen words. My God!

MRS. RIES

Hush! Come with me, then, come and tell me!

SVAVA

No, you don't understand. I didn't mean that. What I have heard shall never pass my lips. No! I must say something to warn these girls. There is one thing we women never learn——

HANNA

What is that?

SVAVA

How easily and how often we deceive ourselves! The greatest precaution is no use.

We are mistaken, again and again! A man folds his arm round you and says: 'I can't bear any one else to touch you!' Gazing into your eyes, as he walks beside you, he says: 'When I see in the ball-room only a flying gleam of your arm, I think, This arm has clung to my neck, and to no other—no other in the whole world!' [*With rising emotion.*] Can she believe, then, that *his* arm has embraced . . . that he . . .

[*She bursts into tears.*

MRS. RIES

Listen to me, Svava!

SVAVA

Don't believe him! He'll only make a fool of you too! [*She draws back.*

MRS. RIES

You have had a dreadful shock, darling. Don't speak of it again.

PETER

There'll be no party *here* to-morrow, you'll see!

SEVERAL

Oh, hold your tongue!

E

PETER

I can see it in her face.   She is in no mood for giving a party.

FREDERIKE

But Svava——?
   [*She looks round for Svava, who has stepped aside.*

HANNA

[*To Mrs. Ries.*]   Auntie, is it true?

KAMMA

[*To Mrs. Ries.*]   Won't there be a party?

ALL

[*Coming near.*]   Oh yes! Oh yes!

MRS. RIES

I hope so.

ALL

[*Surrounding Svava.*]   What about the party?

SVAVA

What do you say?

PETER

You're not in the mood for giving a party here to-morrow, are you?

SVAVA

Oh!—the party! Must we give one to-morrow?   [*Goes up to Mrs. Ries.*

PETER

There! you see!

MRS. RIES

Of course there will be a party.   Of course!

SVAVA

Yes, of course!

ALL

There will be a party! there will be a party! Hurrah!

PETER

Hurrah! So much for their sympathy with Helga Holm! Hurrah!

FREDERIKE

Take care, Peter; you shall pay for that!

ALL

Come: let's throw him out!
                    [*They rush at Peter.*

PETER

No, no: I've an idea.

HANNA

What is it?

PETER

Let's sing the waltz to Svava.   It will put her in good spirits.

ALL

Yes!

MRS. RIES

Oh no, children! don't! Why not take a boat instead, and sing it out there on the water?

ALL THE GIRLS *and* PETER

Oh yes! yes!

PETER

But we'll sing it here, too, that Svava may hear how well it goes already!
  [*He goes to the piano, the girls with him, while the music is distributed.*

SVAVA

[*To Mrs Ries, who is again busy with the flowers.*] Send them away, *do* send them away!

MRS. RIES

Very well!

SVAVA

[*As before.*] There can be no party here to-morrow!

MRS. RIES

Just wait a little!

[*All the girls march out in pairs, led by Peter, in waltz-time, and pass, singing, by Svava and Mrs. Ries. Mrs. Ries makes a sign to Peter to lead the procession out, which he does. The song is heard out-side.*

SVAVA

Oh, my head, my head! I feel as if it were splitting! And yet I've scarcely said a word until just now.

MRS. RIES

You are too excited. You *must* control yourself, my child! You can't stand this!

SVAVA

I shall never have peace again!

MRS. RIES

Where have you been?

SVAVA

Oh, didn't you guess? And *you* talk of a party! You looked so shocked, that you made me say 'yes' too! There can be no question of a party here. Besides, why should we give one now?

MRS. RIES

You surely wouldn't have sent all those children away with such a rebuff? I was on thorns.

SVAVA

Well, it makes no difference to me! Nothing can make any difference now!

MRS. RIES

Yes; but we can't put off the party. We owe it to ourselves as much as to the Christensens! Here comes papa!

SVAVA

Papa too! Well, let him come! . . . though I feel so weak, so dizzy! I can't begin a fight now: but I know well enough what he wants.

THE FOURTH SCENE

As before.   Ries enters from the back.

RIES

[*To Svava.*] Oh! are you there? Why,
Svava, what are you thinking of? [*He comes
nearer.*] Now listen, my dear girl! Let me
tell you, that Mr. Christensen has just telephoned to my office, asking if I am at home.
[*He looks at his watch.*] In a minute he will
be here.

SVAVA

I won't speak to him!
                    [*She makes as if to go away.*

RIES

Very well! But you must stop here and
speak to *me*! Wait a moment! I'm only
going into my room to put away my new hat.
I'm rather dusty, too.   [*Goes into his room.*

MRS. RIES

Of course Mr. Christensen will come! I
quite expected him. If you break off your

engagement with Alf, and for no other reason than this, you will involve the Christensens in a very great scandal. Haven't you realised that?

SVAVA

So it is *I* who will cause the scandal? That's very fine! It's all my fault!

MRS. RIES

The scandal doesn't consist in the thing itself, but in its exposure.

SVAVA

Exactly! exactly!

MRS. RIES

Don't think that so unimportant! One day you will know what it means. It is not so easy to reform the world.

SVAVA

I have no wish to reform it. I only wish to protect myself—that is all!

RIES

[*Coming back.*] Of course, the moment I get home I come in for a bother of this kind. Well, I suppose it couldn't be helped. Indeed, that's your only excuse. Oh! by the way, I just met a man in the street who was at the party last night. He was talking about it. The chief clerk at . . . what's his name? [*To Svava.*] You know him. He owns that charming little place along the fiord—the place you liked so much? [*To Mrs. Ries.*] With the Moorish dovecot . . .?

MRS. RIES

Klinger?

RIES

Ah! Klinger, Klinger. It seems he is anxious to sell it. Oh! and he said: 'You may well feel flattered at your daughter's reception last night; it was a perfect triumph. I pictured her on a high throne, with the whole Christensen family—including "the Dragon"—drawing her chariot.' I assure you, those were his very words. Think of the honour you reflect on us, child! And what a splendid position you will have! . . . And so you want to jump down from your pedestal? Well, you won't get much by that. You will simply fall—smash! before you know where you are. Do you imagine that any well-to-do family anywhere would submit to such an insult, such a slur upon their favourite child? Eh? If you hadn't been suffering from intense excitement, I should have thought you out of your wits to say what you did. And if you take no thought for your own welfare, at least consider ours! On my word, I might just as well have taken a passage to America! I did think of it when I passed the quay and saw the *Angelo* lying ready to sail!

SVAVA

[*Who has hitherto been leaning on the piano, during the following scene alternately moves a few steps towards the back of the stage, and sinks into an easy chair before the piano, keeping her face towards the audience and letting her arms fall over the back of the chair.*]

We had better go to America!

RIES

Better go to America? go to America? A grand idea, isn't it? Such ridiculous nonsense! You seem to think it's as easy to cross the Atlantic as to cross the street. Whatever folly Alf Christensen may have committed—I know nothing about it—it can't have been so *very* bad! [*Svava changes her position at the piano.*] Come, for God's sake, Svava!

SVAVA

Pray, don't drag God's name into it!

RIES

Why not? I should have thought the matter quite serious enough. Doesn't the commandment run: 'Little children, forgive one another'—or something like it? I am not sure of the exact words. We *ought* to forgive one another; we *ought* to help one who has gone astray. It's our duty. Help him to become better . . . by degrees!

MRS. RIES

Ahem!

RIES

Well, it's not my business to preach morality; it sits badly on me, I know. It's very seldom I do. But, all the same, you can't do away with one eternal truth: the woman's duty is to be forbearing to the man, to win him by gentleness and love,—in short, by forbearance. And I don't know any one so admirably adapted for such a work as yourself, Svava. You seem especially gifted. Then again, you have had so much experience—I

mean with children. For it's the same sort of
thing.   In fact, I consider it woman's noblest
vocation !

SVAVA

[*Who has taken up her old position at the
    piano.*
What ?

RIES

What . . . ?   Haven't you been paying atten-
tion ?   Why to . . . to . . . to . . .—you surely
don't need to ask ?—to exert an ennobling
influence through marriage, to make her
husband's life spotless, like . . .

SVAVA

Like soap ?

RIES

Soap ?   Who the devil is talking about
soap ?

MRS. RIES

Ha, ha, ha !

RIES

[*To his wife.*]   Oh, you find that witty ?

SVAVA

It comes to this, then. Marriage is a huge
laundry for men, where we girls are to stand
ready,—each, I suppose, at her wash-tub,
and each with her piece of soap. Is that
what you mean?

MRS. RIES

Ha, ha, ha!

RIES

I don't think it's a subject for laughter.

MRS. RIES

Ha, ha, ha!

RIES

Really, I think these violent attacks on
marriage should be left to the more licentious
sections of society.

SVAVA

To the men, do you mean?

MRS. RIES

Ha, ha, ha!

RIES

Men more licentious than women? Take the women you see at a ball, for instance! With their shoulders bared to the public gaze! And who is the most successful with them? Why, your Don Juans unquestionably! They find such men 'so delightful'! 'so piquant'! Of course! Don't confine your censures to men! You are so taken up with this modern Lamentation over Men, that you forget what the world is like. You forget your own natures. I assure you, you do. [*To Mrs. Ries.*] This is all *your* fault.

MRS. RIES

Mine?

SVAVA

[*Who has been walking up and down, stands still.*

Mother's fault?

RIES

[*To his wife.*] It is the same nonsense your mother always talked. Just the same! And now you have put it into Svava's head! This babble about a 'beast of prey,' and about man's 'freedom to prey on woman,' hindering all other freedom! Is that *never* going to die out?

79

I could answer you if I chose. You count
on my silence.

Well, help me, then, confound it! It's a
matter of life and death for us. We shall all
be turned into the streets if she doesn't mind.

It's not quite so bad as that; although
it is serious, as I told Svava.

Oh, I'm glad of that. And, pray, how am
I to answer Christensen? That's what worries
me. For, with all his elegance and polish,
there's not a more revengeful tiger in the
whole town. His bite is even worse than 'the
Dragon's.' They are not related for nothing.
Am I to say: 'Pardon me, my dear Mr.
Christensen, but my daughter is very sensitive
on this point; she cannot reconcile herself to
the idea that your son actually ventured to
love some one else before he knew her.' Is
that what I'm to say? God knows how I
came to be the father of such a paragon of
virtue!

SVAVA

Bravo! I only beg leave to correct one word.

RIES

Well?

SVAVA

I think you said 'love.'

RIES

Well?

SVAVA

I never reproached Alf with *loving* another woman.

RIES

No?

SVAVA

No, certainly not!

RIES

Oh—ah! I understand! He was—associated —with another woman. Unhappy man! He was associated with another woman before he had the honour and good fortune to know of your existence!

SVAVA

With *one* other ?

RIES

Well, say with two !

SVAVA

With two ?

RIES

Deuce take it ! with several, then ! How everything is buzzed round in this accursed town !

MRS. RIES

Ha, ha, ha !

RIES

Yes : laugh away ! But I ask you in all seriousness—for my part, I find this matter very serious—[*To Svava*] would any one but you be so absurdly unreasonable ? A young man is not to be allowed to take a fancy to any one, until you appear on the scene in all your majestic virtue ? I never met with such arrogance in my life ! Never !

SVAVA

Arrogance ? To claim from another what is expected of yourself ?

MRS. RIES

Ah ! that's the point !

RIES

Yes : that is the point ! Precisely ! You claim the same from man and woman ! Woman, who for centuries has been treated as a man's private property. Of course with men it has been very different ! No : I can't imagine more consummate arrogance ! What the Germans call *hochmuth*, the French *hauteur*, the English——

MRS. RIES

My dear Ries, what is 'marriage' in Turkish ?

RIES

'Marriage' in Turkish ? Oh, I see ! Now I ask you : Is this helping me ? Well, I make you responsible—solely responsible !

MRS. RIES

For ruining her life ?

RIES

Whose ? Svava's ?

SVAVA

[*Who has been seated, rises.*] Do you really wish me to make my home with a man like that?

RIES

What in the world do you mean?

SVAVA

Do you suppose I don't know what it is? Mothers often come to our Orphanage, who need help more than the children. And the tales they tell! To hear them is like gazing down into a black, bottomless hell. Think of what it means, to admit such a pest into a home!

RIES

What are you dreaming of, Svava? Can't you believe that all that sort of thing ceases at marriage? Can't you believe a man's word of honour?

MRS. RIES

Ha, ha, ha!

RIES

Well, well—and if a little slip does occur—

so long as they love each other, . . . and you do love him, don't you, Svava ? You can't deny it. Well, then, simply trust your parents !

[*Svava breaks away to the left. At the same moment the door bell rings.*

MRS. RIES

[*Rising.*] That's Christensen ! I'm going !
[*She tries to follow Svava.*

RIES

No : you are not going ! You mustn't go ! Not both of you ! All right ! Then I shall go too ! [*Approaches her.*

MRS. RIES

[*Holding him back.*] *I* have nothing to say to Christensen !

RIES

And have I ? Have I any part in all this virtue ?

MRS. RIES

Oh ! as to virtue—Christensen and you— you and Christensen—are really *partie égale* !
[*She goes out.*

RIES

De la haute morale ! [*He turns round and advances to the front.*] Yes : a pretty moral, to leave *me* alone to eat up what they've cooked. It's not my fault. I'll be obtuse,— I'll know nothing about it. Yes : that's what I'll do ! If he shows his teeth, I'll show mine ! I shall say straight out : 'I know nothing at all,—haven't heard a word about it !' I'll say : 'The thing can't possibly go any further—if no one has mentioned it even to me.' Yes : I'll say that ; that's what I'll do ! [*The door bell rings again.*] Hullo ! He's still outside ! Ho, ho ! I sha'n't open the door to you, my dear friend ! Stop ! I'll say : 'Let the young folk make it up ! We needn't mind what a woman says when she has lost her temper. Let them make it up themselves !' Yes ; that's the way to look at it ! That's the best thing. I'm quite a diplomatist !

    [*He goes to the piano and plays an ingratiating air.*

THE FIFTH SCENE

Ries.   Christensen.

CHRISTENSEN

[*Enters slowly, and stands still for a moment in the background.*

Bravo, bravo!

RIES

Ah! pardon me! I didn't see you, never heard you come in!

CHRISTENSEN

Pray, don't mention it! Your playing is delightful. There's nothing wrong, then?

RIES

Eh? What do you mean? What should be wrong? Oh! you mean that affair of this morning? That unfortunate business with that clumsy Hoff? Bah! mere woman's chatter! What a woman says or writes on the impulse of the moment needn't be taken *au pied de lettre* —eh? We know, that's soon over. Won't you take a seat?

CHRISTENSEN

Thanks. To-day I've just a twinge in my foot again . . . nothing serious . . . merely a touch . . .

RIES

Gout ?

CHRISTENSEN

Confound you ! don't call it ! It will come at once. There's no danger, then ?

RIES

Not so far as I know ! Let the young folk make it up themselves. Don't you think so ?

CHRISTENSEN

Where are the ladies ?

RIES

I don't know.

CHRISTENSEN

In-deed ? I suppose they knew that I was coming ?

RIES

No—or—rather, yes ! I expect I told them. Aren't you thirsty after your walk ?

CHRISTENSEN

No, thank you. Ahem! ahem! Can it have passed over so quickly?

RIES

Passed over? What? Oh! you mean that affair of this morning? Well, really, I know nothing about it.

CHRISTENSEN

I thought we should have an open rupture, a scandal, and all that!

RIES

Ah! Ha, ha, ha!

CHRISTENSEN

Well, I'm very glad. You are so confident, Mr. Ries. I can't share your feeling at all. These things are dangerous—especially the first time, you know.

RIES

Yes, between married people.

CHRISTENSEN

Oh! between engaged people they're even more dangerous. Once you're married—well,

of course, you *are* married. But in this case
—don't you see? And if there's danger for
Alf, well,—then,—there may be danger for
others as well !

RIES

For others ?

CHRISTENSEN

Yes . . . If such a *very* strong light is thrown
on my son's window, no doubt some of the rays
will fall on mine too. That light—what do
painters call it ?

RIES

Reflected light ?

CHRISTENSEN

Reflected light ! Exactly !

RIES

Ho, ho !

CHRISTENSEN

Yes, laugh away ! You must have your joke.
But, between you and me, what are these ideas
that your daughter has ?

RIES

Shall I tell you exactly ?

CHRISTENSEN

By all means.

RIES

She thinks that a man . . . a man should live
the same life . . .

CHRISTENSEN

Well! well!

RIES

As a girl!—a young girl!

CHRISTENSEN

A man live as strict a life as a young girl?
A man?

RIES

Just so!

CHRISTENSEN

Is she as silly as all that?

RIES

Indeed, she is.

CHRISTENSEN

Ha, ha!

RIES

Ho, ho!

CHRISTENSEN

You must have your joke! You're making fun of me!

RIES

Not at all!

CHRISTENSEN

But the girls of the present day seem to wish just the opposite?

RIES

I've no objection.

CHRISTENSEN

Neither have I. Not that I should care to marry one.

RIES

Whew! No, thank you!

CHRISTENSEN

But now, with regard to your daughter, Mr. Ries. She has been confirmed, hasn't she? And, I suppose, she has been to school, too—what? They learn all sorts of things at school. Her parents' house, of course, has long been recognised as a pattern of good morals. But still, isn't she old enough to read French? Or, in any case, our own literature? These Scandinavian authors don't write for the nursery. And, then, there's this Orphanage, which your daughter founded—didn't she? She must hear all kinds of stories told there by the mothers? And travelled too, hasn't she?

RIES

A good deal.

CHRISTENSEN

Well, there you are! And not with her eyes shut. She had you with her. So she must know *a little* about life, anyhow!

RIES

Yes: and what she didn't know before, she must have learnt by now . . . since she became acquainted with *your* family.

CHRISTENSEN

You mean, that she is in a position to compare . . .?

RIES

Theory with practice. She couldn't have had a better opportunity.

CHRISTENSEN

Hadn't she that already? Well, I'm afraid her reforms will encounter obstacles. Why, you might as well forbid people to eat and drink—eh?

RIES

Ha, ha!

CHRISTENSEN

Ha, ha! Can you imagine, my dear Mr. Ries, the finest and most capable young men in the country (for they are most concerned in this matter) expelled in future from society, and branded as a separate class! All, who— well, who don't endorse your daughter's theory? People demand so much nowadays in the name of morality, that in the end what they demand becomes itself immoral!

RIES

I quite agree with you!

CHRISTENSEN

I knew you would. If people were to take things too seriously—marriage, for example—well, to take only one instance, all the great cities would be ruined. They would collapse, for want of air, like a squeezed india-rubber ball! No, let us make no mistake, my dear Mr. Ries, if your daughter behaves like this, and causes unpleasantness—then—well, then——

RIES

What then?

CHRISTENSEN

Then it will be my turn. I shall begin.

RIES

You? What do you mean?

CHRISTENSEN

She shall have tit for tat.

RIES

You 'll tell her your ideas? I don't understand.

CHRISTENSEN

Not only my ideas. I 'll take care it isn't only on *my* windows that the—what's the painter's name for it?

RIES

The reflected light.

CHRISTENSEN

Yes; I 'll take care the reflected light doesn't only fall on my windows!

RIES

On whose, then?

CHRISTENSEN

I won't say.

RIES

You 're as fond of a joke as ever.

CHRISTENSEN

We both are. However, if you wish to treat it as a joke, you can!

RIES

At whose expense?

CHRISTENSEN

I won't say.

RIES

Well, I can't help what your son did. If you ask me, I think he had better have left it alone, and so had my daughter, instead of making such a stir. For my part, I shall be best pleased if all ends quietly. And that is most likely to happen, in my opinion, if we parents take no more trouble about it.

CHRISTENSEN

You really think so?

RIES

I do.

CHRISTENSEN

Can you guarantee that?

RIES

Guarantee it? How can I?

CHRISTENSEN

Well, that's your affair. *I* must have some security, and, for various reasons, I choose *you*.

RIES

Me?

CHRISTENSEN

There's no peace for the wicked. After the banquet, the bill. Don't you see?

RIES

No, I don't! Such wit is beyond me. And the moral?

CHRISTENSEN

Why, in this bad world innocent people often have to suffer, you know. That is the moral. Do you happen to know Mrs. North?

RIES

Mrs. . . . Mrs. . . . s . . s . . s . .? No!

CHRISTENSEN

Ah! think again! The pretty young widow—the Englishwoman with the pale mother. What? You really can't remember her? And yet I used to see you play duets with her!

RIES

Oh! that woman! of course I know her. I couldn't remember the name, and couldn't quite understand how you came to speak of her just now. Why did you?

CHRISTENSEN

A little while ago she fell into some money difficulties—such as may happen to the best of us. She is rather gay, you know—lives in great style—and at that time she did me the honour to pay me a visit. *You* were not at home just then.

RIES

I ? I never had anything to do with Mrs. North's money-matters.

CHRISTENSEN

I only wished to pay you a compliment. Your gallantry to ladies is so widely recognised, you know, that, had you been in the town, of course she would have come to you—with whom she used to play duets—not to me. That was all I meant. What did you think I meant ?

RIES

Mean what you like ! What have Mrs. North's money-matters to do with me ?

CHRISTENSEN

She is going abroad !

RIES

Indeed !

CHRISTENSEN

She 's coming here to say good-bye.

RIES

[*Springs up.*] Coming here?

CHRISTENSEN

Yes. She used to come here often enough
. . . at one time. When you used to play
duets together.

RIES

Not latterly.

CHRISTENSEN

I wasn't aware of that. She said nothing to
me about it. We made an appointment to
meet—she and I—here.

RIES

You and Mrs. North? To meet here?
Now?

CHRISTENSEN

She is going on board to-night. The
Angelo is lying ready to sail.

RIES

Of course I shall be pleased to see Mrs.
North. It can't matter to me. I have
nothing against her. But I don't see why

my wife should meet her here, if she doesn't wish it. And she certainly doesn't. Therefore Mrs. North can't come. It is impossible.

CHRISTENSEN

Well, but your wife isn't at home ? Surely *you* can receive her ?

RIES

Impossible ! Suppose my wife came in ? They mustn't meet on any account.

CHRISTENSEN

Well, shall I . . . ?

RIES

Oh dear no ! But, of course, if Mrs. North does come, you won't mind my going out to induce her to go away ?

CHRISTENSEN

Of course not. [*He rises.*] So you, too, are afraid of the reflected light ?

RIES

Not in the least. I am simply considering my wife.

CHRISTENSEN

That's really very nice of you. It isn't every one who does that. [*The door bell rings.*] There she is—I believe—already.

RIES

Mrs. North? Impossible!
[*He rushes to the window.*

CHRISTENSEN

I've often noticed how punctual she is. English, you know!
[*He goes to the other window.*

RIES

[*At the window.*] Yes, by Jove! there she is!

CHRISTENSEN

Of course you will let her in at once.

RIES

Excuse me! On no account. I must prevent it. [*He hastens to the door.*

CHRISTENSEN

[*At the window.*] Hallo! why, your wife *is* at home.

RIES

[*Standing still.*] My wife? Where is she?

CHRISTENSEN

Down there! She is just meeting Mrs. North.

RIES

My wife? Mrs. . . . ?

CHRISTENSEN

Yes! there she goes, full sail!

RIES

Really! really! Is she at home, after all? Dear me! What will happen next? [*Muttering.*] An earthquake?

CHRISTENSEN

[*As before.*] Why, your daughter is at home too!

RIES

My daughter too . . . where?

CHRISTENSEN

Down there as well. Your wife has stepped forward a little, your daughter is stopping still. Won't you convince yourself?

RIES

Oh no! Thank you, thank you! No! Let's leave them alone! Let's leave them alone! I shall enter a monastery! A monastery's the place for me! No. I'll go to the piano instead! I'll plunge head over heels into a waltz!

[*Flings himself on the stool in front of the piano, and plays a furious waltz.*

THE SIXTH SCENE

As before. Mrs. Ries, white as a sheet and speechless, enters hastily from the back.

CHRISTENSEN

We are having a little music, Mrs. Ries.

MRS. RIES

Mrs. North is here.

RIES

[*Without leaving off.*] Oh, is that you?
[*He begins to sing.*

CHRISTENSEN

Your husband has a fine touch. And a good voice, too!

MRS. RIES

Mrs. North is here!

RIES

What? Who? Oh—ah! Mrs. North! [*He rises.*] In half a minute, I'll . . . My dear, what can she want here? [*He goes to the door, but turns back.*] Oh! my hat! I beg your pardon! [*Goes into his room. At this moment the Trio is heard in the distance. He comes back.*] Ah! the Trio! How lovely music sounds on the water! Now what can this woman want from me?

[*Retires by right to the back.*

CHRISTENSEN

[*To Mrs Ries.*] How lucky that I was able to see you! Your husband had no idea you were at home!

MRS. RIES

[*Goes up to him.*] This is *your* work!

CHRISTENSEN

What do you mean?

MRS. RIES

Mrs. North's visit.

CHRISTENSEN

To say good-bye ?

MRS. RIES

Y̆ou know the secret of this house. And you intend to use it against us.

[*She bursts into tears. Svava enters quickly, and in great astonishment, by the right, from the back, as though to seek an explanation, but stops still when she observes that Christensen is still there, and sees that Mrs. Ries is crying; she withdraws noiselessly, through the second door on the left.*

CHRISTENSEN

I and mine wish for nothing better than to live on good terms with you and yours. You know that quite well. But if your daughter persists in bringing disgrace, perhaps calamity, on all of us—for my son takes the matter greatly to heart—why, in that case, Mrs. Ries, in that case . . .

MRS. RIES

You are a wicked man !

CHRISTENSEN

And a good man. Both together. I only wish to say this: If you expose my son, I'll expose your husband!

MRS. RIES

What barbarity! [*Svava is heard to utter a shriek.*] Svava!
[*She sinks into a chair.*

CHRISTENSEN

[*After a pause.*] I didn't wish that! I didn't intend that! [*In going out.*] However, *enfin!* [1]
[*Passes by the right to the back.*

THE SEVENTH SCENE

Mrs. Ries. Svava enters slowly from the left.

MRS. RIES

[*Moves a few steps forward, then stops still.*] Listen to me, before you judge, listen to me!

[1] At the representation in Christiania the Second Act closes with the Sixth Scene, with Christensen's '*Enfin!*'

SVAVA

[*Waves her aside with a gesture of the hand
and head, goes straight to the table, sits
down before it, lays her arm on the table,
and leans her head on her arm, while she
stares fixedly in front of her.*

This is too much in one day!

MRS. RIES

Let me explain to you. Let me tell you——
[*She stops short.*

SVAVA

Oh no! Let me be alone!
[*Mrs. Ries goes out silently, after looking
back several times.*

MEANWHILE THE CURTAIN FALLS.

THE THIRD ACT

*The same room on the next morning, decorated with
flowers for the party. The table on the right is
laid for breakfast for two persons.*

THE FIRST SCENE

*Mrs. Ries and Mrs. Christensen enter from the
back; the latter in a hat and with a shawl over
her arm, which Mrs. Ries takes from her. Enter
later, Marie.*

MRS. CHRISTENSEN

It was extremely kind of you to see me. I
am sure you must be very busy.

MRS. RIES

And I am so grateful to you for coming. I
wanted to have a talk with you.

MRS. CHRISTENSEN

Well, what do you say to our having the
party here to-day—after all? Do you know,
I'm sure it's the best thing to do? If the
engagement is to be broken off, at any rate, it
mustn't be in this way.

MRS. RIES

I thoroughly agree with you.

MRS. CHRISTENSEN

Think of the gossip it would cause! Two days after the engagement had been announced!

MRS. RIES

Still, it is very trying for Svava.

MRS. CHRISTENSEN

Of course. But she need only show herself and say she is unwell. By the way, your husband asked to be remembered to you.

MRS. RIES

Has he been round to see you already?

MRS. CHRISTENSEN

He came expressly to fetch Alf. What an amusing man your husband is!

MRS. RIES

And your son had no objection?

MRS. CHRISTENSEN

How can you ask? If we're to have the party, of course the young folk must have a talk together first!

MRS. RIES

So we thought!

MRS. CHRISTENSEN

Of course! She takes it more sensibly, I hear, to-day.

MRS. RIES

As regards the party, yes. Won't you sit down?

MRS. CHRISTENSEN

[*Seats herself.*] Thank you. What does she say, Mrs. Ries?

MRS. RIES

I 've scarcely spoken to her myself. I 've not had a chance yet; I 've so much depending on me to-day. What a blessing it is that we still have old Marie with us!

> [*Marie enters at this moment with the chocolate.*

MRS. CHRISTENSEN

Good morning, Marie!

MARIE

Good morning, Mrs. Christensen!

MRS. CHRISTENSEN

How is Miss Ries?

MARIE

Thank you, she was not at all well yesterday—after Mr. Christensen called.

MRS. CHRISTENSEN

Christensen ? Did he call yesterday?

MARIE

Yesterday evening.

MRS. CHRISTENSEN

Yesterday evening? My husband?

MRS. RIES

He just dropped in to see Ries.

MRS. CHRISTENSEN

Indeed? He said nothing about it.

MARIE

[*While she fills the cups.*] I think she takes it more sensibly to-day. She cries a good deal still; but she went for her bath, and ate a little breakfast. Now she's out for a .walk.

MRS. RIES

Pray, help yourself!

MRS. CHRISTENSEN

[*Leans forward.*] Thanks! What does she-say, Marie?

MARIE

She doesn't say much. But she's more resigned to the idea of the party.

MRS. CHRISTENSEN

Is she?

MARIE

She thinks the party cannot be put off.

MRS. CHRISTENSEN

Of course not!

MARIE

She quite sees that. I told her so myself.

MRS. RIES

Won't you try this cake? It's a specialty.

MRS. CHRISTENSEN

[*Taking it.*] Thanks very much! What does she say about Alf?

MARIE

She said to-day: 'Perhaps I've been un-just to him.'

MRS. CHRISTENSEN

Ah, indeed she has, Marie. So she sees that now?

MARIE

And then she began to cry. I didn't like to bother her any more.

MRS. CHRISTENSEN

Thank you, Marie, thank you! [*Marie goes out.*] Aren't you pleased? You hear what Marie says?

MARIE

[*Turns round.*] What?

MRS. CHRISTENSEN

I didn't call you: I only mentioned your name.

MARIE

Oh, I see! [*She goes out.*

MRS. CHRISTENSEN

You are upset, Mrs. Ries. I should so like to have a little talk with you. We mothers understand these things so much better than men.

MRS. RIES

I thought that too.

MRS. CHRISTENSEN

May I?

MRS. RIES

[*Helping her.*] I beg your pardon? I'm forgetting everything!

MRS. CHRISTENSEN

Your cake is delicious. As to what happened yesterday, of course it was awfully unpleasant—that affair with Hoff. To think that he should have the impertinence! This is how it came about: Miss Tang—I think you knew Miss Tang?—used to live with us. But Christensen is so strict: he won't have anything of that sort in the house. So we had to send Alf away—and she got married. I assure you, Mrs. Ries, no one was any the wiser. Alf is so discreet in these matters—

you wouldn't believe how discreet he is.   If Hoff hadn't found those tiresome letters, he would never have known anything.   And Christensen will soon put that to rights, you may be quite sure ! No one knows a word about it : that's the great thing, Mrs. Ries.   Men will be men, and we can't alter them.

MRS. RIES

Ah, if Mrs. Hoff's were the only case !

MRS. CHRISTENSEN

But surely there are no others ?

MRS. RIES

Indeed there are.   Yesterday afternoon Svava went straight off to Miss Honoria Christensen.

MRS. CHRISTENSEN

To 'the Dragon'? My dear Mrs. Ries, what a thing to do !

MRS. RIES

And there she learned a great deal.

MRS. CHRISTENSEN

Oh ! but you mustn't believe her, Mrs Ries. Every one knows 'the Dragon.' Once she was taken in herself, and she has made a dead set at all engagements ever since ; it's a well-known fact ! She has made a good deal of mischief before now ; she's a spiteful woman.

MRS. RIES

Spiteful she may be, but she's not a liar.

MRS. CHRISTENSEN

The Christensens are not in the habit of lying. But, Mrs. Ries, ... she may be misinformed by others !

MRS. RIES

All this has shocked my daughter terribly.

MRS. CHRISTENSEN

Of course. Isn't 'the Dragon' detestable ? She almost hates Alf—and do you know why ? Because he has such a good reputation.

MRS. RIES

Yes, he has.

MRS. CHRISTENSEN

Indeed he has !

MRS. RIES

Still, he has been rather wild, hasn't he, however discreet? . . . And, if a man doesn't resist temptation early in life, but gives way time after time, you can't expect him to have much character, can you?

MRS. CHRISTENSEN

No : you 're quite right ! [*She reaches across the table.*] You must forgive me! I have had no breakfast yet. I have got into the bad habit of lying very late in the morning.

MRS. RIES

Please help yourself! I didn't say that because I expect any more from your son than from others.

MRS. CHRISTENSEN

No, most young men are alike. Just fancy, Mrs. Ries, I knew nothing about such things when I married.

MRS. RIES

We didn't know much in those days; or, if we did, we thought no more about it. However, many of us had all the more to learn afterwards, Mrs. Christensen.

MRS. CHRISTENSEN

Don't speak of it!

MRS. RIES

I think we ought to speak of it more than ever, for it's just that which concerns us now.

MRS. CHRISTENSEN

Oh, I must tell you something! The other day I was looking through a history belonging to my daughter—she's a student, you know. I read there that the bridal costume—the white robe, the veil, and all that—is nothing but the old sacrificial dress, handed down from the time when human beings were offered up to Moloch. The same is true of the wreath, worn by the innocent victims. It made me cry, Mrs. Ries. , [*Marie comes in with a small bottle of champagne.*] O my dear Mrs. Ries——!

MRS. RIES

I'm told that now and then at breakfast you——

MRS. CHRISTENSEN

True. But why should you take so much trouble? Still, you wouldn't believe what good champagne does, when you have had no sleep. And, I expect, neither you nor I slept particularly well last night.

[*Marie, who meanwhile has poured out the champagne and filled up the glasses, goes out.*

MRS. RIES

[*Offering a glass to Mrs. Christensen.*] Allow me.

MRS. CHRISTENSEN

Let's drink this toast: That all may come right again!

MRS. RIES

Yes: I could wish for nothing better. If only——

MRS. CHRISTENSEN

Oh, you may be quite easy. Alf has such a refined nature.

MRS. RIES

Is he true?

MRS. CHRISTENSEN

True as steel! [*They drink.*] You must drink it all! Else it won't do you good.

MRS. RIES

Yes, I really think——

[*She empties her glass and fills up Mrs. Christensen's.*

MRS. CHRISTENSEN

Of course, one mustn't be unjust, either—I mean, to men. For, after all, such men generally make the best husbands, Mrs. Ries. We can't deny that.

MRS. RIES

They make us comfortable, do you mean?

MRS. CHRISTENSEN

Yes, and treat their wives with respect. It is so, as a rule.

MRS. RIES

They are very obliging.

MRS. CHRISTENSEN

Most obliging, and much more attentive than other husbands. Let us give them their due.

MRS. RIES

Still, it is not right of wives to condone——

MRS. CHRISTENSEN

No, it's not right. But so it is, whether we like it or not. If I may, I'll take another piece of cake. It is really delicious.

MRS. RIES

Do! May I fill up your glass?

MRS. CHRISTENSEN

Thanks, only a little. We women have so much to put up with, so much, that taxes our strength. [*She drinks.*] Still, on the other hand, we have many consolations, too. A man may have faults, and yet be a real treasure in other respects—don't you think?

MRS. RIES

Yes. Only my mother said once to . . . well, to a friend of mine—(it's a long while ago now) . . . —she said: 'Let him be the ablest man in the whole town: you will be none the happier, if he isn't faithful.'

MRS. CHRISTENSEN

You are so upset to-day, Mrs. Ries. You have had no sleep. Come, drink a little more wine, to keep me company. It will do you good. May I? [*She takes the bottle and pours the rest of the wine into Mrs. Ries's glass—and her own.*] The chaplain very often calls about this time in the morning. And then we sit and chat together, just as you and I are doing now. [*She takes her glass.*] Well, may everything end happily, Mrs. Ries! [*They drink.*]

MRS. RIES

I can't finish it.

MRS. CHRISTENSEN

No? Then—if you'll excuse me—I will. One so soon feels at home with you, Mrs. Ries. You must come to see me oftener. About this time is the best. I suppose you go to hear the chaplain's sermons, don't you?

MRS. RIES

No; I haven't cared about going to church lately.

MRS. CHRISTENSEN

Oh! but you should. If we hadn't the consolation of religion, Mrs. Ries! I'm sure, very often, I don't know where . . .

The Second Scene

As before. Ries.

RIES

[*Comes in from the back with a furled flag in his hand, which he puts down on the right, and then steps to the front.*

Look here !

MRS. CHRISTENSEN

Back already ?

RIES

Yes, and I brought Alf: I only waited till he had finished dressing. I wished him to come before Svava returns. It is best they should meet out of doors. She can't help speaking to him then ; she can't very well run away from him.

MRS. CHRISTENSEN

You are quite right. In fact, you generally are.

RIES

Thank you, much obliged. [*To his wife.*] Do you hear that?

MRS. CHRISTENSEN

This meeting between our dear children is of great importance to us all.

RIES

Of the greatest importance! But I'm disturbing you.

MRS. CHRISTENSEN

Not at all, not at all! I was only anxious that we mothers might have a little chat together. Of course we have had most experience.

RIES

Naturally.

MRS. CHRISTENSEN

I tell your wife that marriage doesn't consist only of love, but of many other things as well. Am I right?

RIES

I should think so! And a marriage with your son——

MRS. CHRISTENSEN

Oh, I never said that!

RIES

Why shouldn't you? It is only word for word what I was saying yesterday. I can tell you that without flattering you or your son.

MRS. CHRISTENSEN

When you think it is a choice between making such a match—well, as your daughter can make—and becoming an embittered old maid like 'the Dragon'!—Ugh!

RIES

Ugh! Do you know a favourite saying of mine?: If virtue is not to decay, it must be preserved by matrimony. Just as fruit . . .

MRS. CHRISTENSEN

Ha, ha, ha! I never thought we should laugh to-day. Let's take it for a good omen! May we often meet and laugh together in future! Good-bye! for I really must go now. The whole family is assembled in our house.

RIES

So I hear.

MRS. CHRISTENSEN

We shall come in ever so many boats, with singing and playing, for we have a whole

orchestra amongst us.   Pray, don't give your-
selves the trouble!   No, really I can't allow it!
                    [*Ries and Mrs. Ries follow her out.*

RIES

[*Coming back at once.*]   Truly, I'm as tired
. . . of all this worry and suspense, as if I had
spent the whole morning on the treadmill—
and the whole night too !
> [*Mrs. Ries comes back, and passes Ries
> without looking at him.   Ries stands
> considering a moment, then goes towards
> his room, but stops still before the
> door.*

I bought a large new flag to-day.   And I
carried it home myself.   Here it is.   [*He
fetches it.   After a pause :*]   Isn't it time for us
to dress ?

MRS. RIES

I have put out everything ; I can be ready
in a few minutes.

RIES

So have I, only . . . [*He moves a step, then
stands still again.*]   Oh! did I tell you that
Klinger wishes to sell his villa out there ?   Or
did I forget ?

MRS. RIES

No; you told me.

RIES

To-day I telephoned to ask how much he
would sell it for. There is a garden attached,
and a little wood—quite a small one. He wants
30,000 kroner. That's not dear——what?

MRS. RIES

No; not if one had the means——

RIES

Well, but we have the means.

MRS. RIES

We have? What should *we* want with a
place out there?

RIES

Not ourselves, perhaps. Svava might like it.

MRS. RIES

Svava?

RIES

You know she has taken a great fancy to
that house—and the situation is splendid! We
shall pass the place to-day. Still, if you don't

care for the idea, of course——I have got my trunks at last. You really ought to look at them now. I mean at my presents. No? Oh! well then, I'll go and dress! [*Goes out.*

THE THIRD SCENE

Mrs. Ries. Svava comes in by the left near the foreground.

MRS. RIES

[*Startled.*] Are you there? They said you had gone out. Have you met no one?

SVAVA

Whom should I have met?

> [*Mrs. Ries is silent. Svava takes off her hat and puts it on the piano, then goes forward and seats herself on a low chair on the left and begins to draw off her gloves.*

I haven't felt able to talk to any one—least of all to you. But now I would like so much to try, if you don't mind?

MRS. RIES

No. [*Pause.*

SVAVA

I don't quite know how to begin; there's
so much to say. But, I wish—I wish, first
of all, to ask one question: How long have
you known this? [*Mrs. Ries is silent. Gently :*]
I'm sorry I asked. Only you can't wonder
at my feeling upset. How could I be
so terribly mistaken? Once before, and now
again. I seem to have been brought up
to make mistakes. I don't mean that as
a reproach; I only mean that I'm not to
blame myself. And yet, when I think how
grandly I talked, and how severe I was!
How could you let me? How could you be
so cruel?

MRS. RIES

I gave you several hints, but they only made
you more excited. As lately as yesterday . . .

SVAVA

I'm beginning to see many things since
yesterday. Perhaps this, too, will become clear,

I

. . . one day. I only know that since yesterday everything at home here has grown bitter
to me—everything—even the sound of the
piano! [*Pause.*] This is what you meant,
then, when you warned me not to be so
arrogant. I was to stoop as low as I could.
You must stoop very low to be on a level with
life.

MRS. RIES

O Svava!

SVAVA

There is one safe rule. Do as the rest of
the world! Then we have no right to com-
plain.

MRS. RIES

No; but . . .

SVAVA

[*As before.*] To think that I never understood that before! I was like a simple child.
I stood before a high mountain and wanted to
push it away with my hands.

MRS. RIES

Yes.

SVAVA

Still, one can go right away from it all. One can always do that. Why didn't you, mother ? Since yesterday I understand what you have suffered, and yet you didn't go away. Why didn't you—at once—the same day? That first day must have been the hardest of all. I shall never understand.

MRS. RIES

Don't say that, Svava !

SVAVA

I shall never understand ! You are thinking of papa? Ah! . . . he is so kind-hearted, so lovable ! No; I cannot speak of papa.

[*She bursts into tears.*

MRS. RIES

No one can realise it who hasn't had the experience ! I mean, what it is possible to endure, when a house rests, like ours, on a secret. And the ingenuity which must be employed to conceal it ! Oh, if you only knew to what I have descended ! At last all one's ambition is swallowed up in a single aim : to know that the secret is well guarded. All else is nothing.

SVAVA

But why act as you did? I don't wish to utter a word of reproach, but had it been the one whom *I* loved most in the world, then I could have borne it least of all!

MRS. RIES

You don't know what you are saying.

SVAVA

Don't I? If he were even more, if he were the best, the noblest . . . oh, no! it would have been simply impossible; in such a case the discovery would have driven me mad.

MRS. RIES

Suppose I only bore it for the sake of my child.

SVAVA

[*As though a light suddenly struck her, throws herself into her mother's arms.*
O mother! I . . .

MRS. RIES

Hush! You were quite little then, and I didn't dare alone . . .

SVAVA

Hush, hush!

[*Mrs. Ries sinks into a chair, Svava kneels
down before her, and buries her head in
her lap.*

The Fourth Scene

As before.   Ries.

RIES

[*Comes out of his room in frock-coat and white
tie, and approaches them, with back half
turned towards them.*

I say, this coat doesn't seem to fit well,
does it?   At the side here?   Or, perhaps, the
back's not quite right—just here?   What do
you think?   Is the lower part all right?   The
idea of a famous Parisian firm turning out an
article of this sort!   What are we coming to?
And I was so certain of my bargain!   It never
does to be so confident.   [*He notices Svava,
who has risen and moved towards the left.*]   Are
you there?   I thought you had gone out.   I
sent Alf to meet you.   They said you had
gone down to the shore.   So you hadn't, after

all? By the way, Svava! I was just speaking to mother about . . . don't you remember that villa of Klinger's? We shall pass it to-day—we shall pass it to-day. However, we can talk about that later. [*Goes to the back.*] But now I must really use the little time we have left to show you what I brought with me from Paris. [*While he enters his room.*] I have all the things ready, so it won't take more than a second. I will bring them all at once. [*He goes out.*

SVAVA

I am going.

MRS. RIES

No: don't go!

SVAVA

But I can't bear it.

MRS. RIES

Svava! what do you think I have had to bear?

RIES

[*From the next room.*] Here I come!
[*He comes out with a huge garden-hat on his head, and two shawls over his shoulders.*

Two fans with long cords hang from his
button-hole. He carries under his arms
several parcels, in his hands bundles of
dress materials and more parcels.

Now, you really can't say I think only of
myself when I travel. If any one imagines
that all these things are to be had at one and
the same shop—well, he knows nothing at all
about them. No, they deserve long and care-
ful inspection. What do you say to this
garden-hat? [*He takes it from his head.*] A
smart fellow, isn't he? [*He lays it aside.*]
But now in these parcels—[*Opening them.*]
'Beware of thine heart, for out of the heart
come vain thoughts'—isn't that how it
runs?—two, elegant, elegant——look! [*He ex-
hibits two ladies' hats.*] Mother and daughter!
Here is the mother—[*He holds one of them up.*]
—soft in tone, serious, like a moss rose with
closed petals; the daughter, dazzling, fresh,
and a little giddy. Can't you imagine these
two hats, jesting together in a box at the
theatre? Between the acts of ' On ne badine
pas avec l'amour' ? And these two fans—eh ?
A discreet accompaniment to the ladies'
thoughts. This, in colour and movement,
conveys a certain suggestion of motherly pride
—so! [*He fans himself.*] And this protests
with some little vehemence against 'his'

having the assurance to pay attentions to another lady—so! [*He fans himself.*] Imagine it's a warm summer evening! Such a fan as this is as expressive as a guitar—piano, pizzicato! [*He fans himself.*] But, now, what do you say to my dress-materials? With a dress made of this—[*He names colour and material.*]—mother will look like a day in early September—the loveliest and most temperate season in the whole year.

> [*Svava can suppress her feelings no longer. He packs his things hastily together and carries as much as can be dragged into his room.*

MRS. RIES

You mustn't take it to heart so! Or I shall give way too! [*Begins to cry.*

SVAVA

No, I'll try! I'll try! But—— [*Again bursts into tears.*

MRS. RIES

This will never do!

SVAVA

I will control myself soon!

MRS. RIES

If you can't, we must put off the party.

SVAVA

No, no! Anything rather than that. Trust to me.

RIES

[*Comes out of his room.*] I see Alf coming. [*With a glance at Svava.*] Shall I ask him to go away?

MRS. RIES

I don't think it is necessary.

•

RIES

He may come, then? [*Svava nods assent.*] Oh thank you, darling!
[*He involuntarily takes a few steps towards Svava, then stops still, and withdraws silently through the door on the right.*

MRS. RIES

I will put everything out for you, and then send Marie to help you. [*Svava goes up to her.*] Try now to control yourself.
[*She goes out by the second door on the left.*

The Fifth Scene

Svava. Alf in frock-coat, etc., enters on the right. Last of all, Ries. Svava draws back to the extreme left.

ALF

[*Goes a few steps towards her.*] I suppose you know why I have come? If it rested with me, I would gladly have spared you. But if we are to be together at the party, we had better settle what line to take.

SVAVA

Yes.

ALF

I thought, if you have no objection, I would help your father to receive the guests. I could be a kind of steward, or something of that sort, so as to superintend the party from the first. Your father likes the idea. In that way I should be fully occupied, and we need seldom meet. Have you any objection?

SVAVA

No.

ALF

If, however, we are forced to meet, I'll
soon remember something or other which has
been forgotten. But I can't release you from
the first dance.

SVAVA

No, that is clear.

ALF

I will try not to prolong your suffering. I
will even try to be amusing!

SVAVA

Yes, you must have a double share of good
spirits.

ALF

In such a case one can generally carry it
through. I will do my best. But you must
try as well.

SVAVA

It's not quite the same for me.

ALF

I propose that you simply copy me, and put off the serious part until after the party.

SVAVA

Haven't we done with that? Is there still more to come?

ALF

Yes; I certainly wish to defend myself! You surely won't condemn me unheard?

SVAVA

I *have* heard. At any rate I wish to hear no more.

ALF

I dare say you don't wish to hear, but you must, for all that. Even a criminal is not sentenced without a hearing.

SVAVA

I had no intention of sentencing any one.

ALF

You *have* passed sentence, I can see.

SVAVA

In that case my sentence has evidently done you no harm. You seem as unabashed as ever!

ALF

Of course you expected me to appear before you in the character of a penitent sinner? To fall at your feet with tears and contrition, and ask your forgiveness? You must really excuse me! That would simply be admitting that you had confided in one who is unworthy of you, and that slight I will not inflict on you or myself. I certainly do not believe that I am unworthy of you. Had I thought so I would never have come here.

SVAVA

You have come here, then, with nothing on your conscience?

ALF

I won't say that; I may have had many things on my conscience. But at present they lie behind me; my hands are clean.

SVAVA

Really! Since when, may I ask?

ALF

That is no business of yours. But I can tell you of one day in my life which had tremendous consequences for me, and that was the day when I met you.

SVAVA

No doubt I ought to feel flattered. You have nothing on your conscience, then. Nothing to explain.

ALF

Plenty to explain! But, as I said before, we had better drop the subject for the present.

SVAVA

I think so too : we will drop the subject.

ALF

Until you learn what is involved in this question.

SVAVA

No, at once !

ALF

Yes, for you don't understand in the least.

This is not a question simply of myself or any other individual ; therefore, you have no right to pass sentence. Least of all, can you put all the blame on me. That would be the most glaring injustice. Besides, it can't be helped : we must accept facts, as they are. I see you don't understand. However, when you have learnt to look into the question (and now it is *your duty* to look into it), then, and not before, it will be time enough for me to relate to you this little episode of mine, if you insist. I know beforehand that you will then trouble yourself no more about it.

SVAVA

It's not that which troubles me now. You have quite misunderstood me. I am ashamed that you should have thought I meant that!

ALF

If I have hurt your feelings, I beg you to remember that I feel hurt too.

SVAVA

You? I suppose, because I won't put up with it ?

ALF

You have nothing to put up with. If my past were not honourable, I should not stand here.

SVAVA

We differ on that point. And you have known that from the first.

ALF

Oh, that's it! I have deceived you, have I? Been false to you? Perhaps I have been laughing at you in my sleeve all laong?

SVAVA

Is that all you can say?

ALF

You interfere in my private affairs; I feel hurt. You mistrust me; that hurts me too. . . . But, I beg you, let us postpone all this!

SVAVA

If it had been I? If *I* had come to you under similar circumstances? 'My private affairs.' 'I feel hurt.' 'You mistrust me, and that hurts me too.' Suppose I had behaved as *you* have, lived the life you have lived?

RIES

[*Outside.*] I see the boats putting in. We shall have them here in a minute! [*He enters.*] How are things going, children?

SVAVA

Exactly as they ought.

RIES

No; really? It's all being cleared up?

SVAVA

Completely.

RIES

No? I *am* glad! You both look in high spirits, too. I was sure you only wanted a few words together. Besides, who can doubt a man's word of honour?

[*He plunges on to the stool in front of the piano, plays a few rapid bars of a Triumphal March, then rushes into his room.*

ALF

This is too bad! You know quite well that there was no question of such theories when we were engaged. I thought as little of my past as you of yours. Ever since our first long talk together we have belonged to

each other. You know it was so. I see you
can't deny it. As for my past, it can't have
been very dreadful. It can't have left any
deep traces; else you—*you* especially—would
have avoided me instinctively. Instead of
that you felt drawn to me more strongly than
to any other. I have it from your own lips;
you told me so yourself. Our present relations
are unnatural; you are not yourself; we are
both in a false position. If only I might
speak to you, as I believe I can speak, I should
convince you on the spot.

SVAVA

Do you think so?

ALF

Do I think so? I'm sure of it! Else I
should not have been so confident from the
first—nor so confident now. If I trusted you
too implicitly—well, that is a fault, which you
must try to forgive! But my trust was not
misplaced; I know you too well. Although
we have only been such a short time together,
I know you as well,—nay, better—than any
one else in the whole world! You told me
that, too, with your own lips. [*Svava is moved.*]
I see you remember! What is the matter
with you, Svava?

SVAVA

You have not answered my question. O God! O God!

ALF

Let us keep to the point. You must answer me first. How can any one, who knows you as thoroughly as I, wish to deceive you, to be false to you? You ought to have more faith in me.

SVAVA

This is too much! If it had been I—would you have had faith in me?

ALF

How can I tell? You wouldn't have been yourself—but some one else.

SVAVA

Well, that is just what you have become— some one else! That is the dreadful part of it!

ALF

Hush, hush! You shall soon see that I am the same, just the same! And besides, you wouldn't feel it so deeply if you really thought me different.

[*The Trio is heard in the distance.*

RIES

[*Comes out of his room and speaks in a whisper.*] The Trio! Do you hear it? I have forgotten the flag. [*He quickly crosses the room, takes the furled flag, and hastens out by left.*] I hope I shall be able to unfurl the thing easily, else . . .

[*Goes out. Svava takes up her hat and gloves.*

ALF

You're not going? Just when the music reminds us of all our happiness during the last few days? Think of what *really* brought us together. Surely *that* was no mistake. The work we resolved to carry on together; the work we talked over so often. Can you live without it? *I* can't; and I see you can't either. Let us devote our future to it. In that work I find my real self. You once told me so, and you were quite right.

SVAVA

How can I reconcile the two? As long as I live, I shall never understand how a man can be so double. It is horrible!

ALF

Haven't we all two natures, then?

SVAVA

Two——?

ALF

Yes; you, as much as I. Why do you look
at me like that? I know what I'm saying.
We were attracted to each other by natural
affinity,—an affinity so strong as to annul any
tendencies in which we differed. Did you
ever shrink from me? No: you felt drawn
towards me. Now you are hiding your real
self, and that is why you are misled. You
ought to be on your guard against these
absurd theories, not against me.

SVAVA

No—no, this is too much! Even if it were
true, you have no right to use such words to
me. I have not two natures, and I will never
belong to a man who can stoop to be so double.
[*Both come more and more to the front.*

ALF

Don't you suppose that whenever I drew you
to me I could tell how willing you were? A

man cannot help knowing what influence he has over a woman.

SVAVA

Not another word!

ALF

Yes; you can't deny it! To renounce your own nature now would be as great a sin as any I have committed

SVAVA

You revolt me!

ALF

Are you still so deeply stirred by a word from me? You see—how entirely you are mine! I know it, you know it yourself. Only yesterday——

SVAVA

Do you dare to remind me of yesterday?

ALF

Dare? Only yesterday—here, on this very spot—you proved to me that you have two natures;—you changed colour; you trembled, when I said that your arm had clung to my neck, and to no other, no other in the whole world!

SVAVA

Yes !—and yours to a hundred others !

[*She flings her glove in his face and rushes off*
towards the left. Alf stands dazed for a
moment and then hastens off by the right to
the back.

RIES

[*Coming out of his room.*] I congratulate you!
I congratulate you !

[*He stands astonished, moves forward, and*
casts a puzzled look on all sides. As he
turns round.

THE CURTAIN FALLS.